TABLE OF CONTENTS

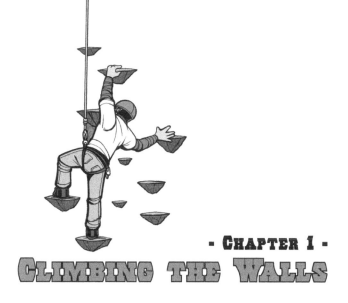

CHAPTER 1

CLIMBING THE WALLS

Amir leaned against the cold, hard surface. A drop of sweat ran down his forehead, slid down his cheek, and dripped off the end of his chin. Amir's eyes darted down. He watched the bead of sweat fall to the ground far below.

Suddenly, Amir was beginning to feel like he might lose his grip at any moment. It didn't help that the surface he was climbing was completely vertical.

There was no place to rest. There wasn't even a way to pause to wiggle his hands or feet to keep them from hurting.

Amir felt his breathing pick up. He was trying hard to keep control of his muscles. After all, he was just a few feet away from climbing higher than he had ever reached before.

If he reached the point he was seeking, it would be incredible. But if he failed, Amir would fall. To make matters worse, if he did fall, the ground below was solid and hard. It would not be a soft landing.

It was not his first free climb. Amir did have experience climbing without any ropes, but he had never climbed this high before.

Amir paused for as long as he could.

Slowly, he looked up, trying to find something to hold on to. He had to figure out something that he could hold on to next. Just a few inches above his right hand, he saw it. There was a nice gripping point that he could hold on to.

He looked down below for a place to adjust his feet. There was a better hold for his right foot. Amir knew that he'd have to release his right-handed grip and his right foot at the same time to move without falling.

That wasn't the way an experienced climber would do it. A real free climber moved slowly and carefully. He or she moved one step at a time, never taking any unnecessary risks. But Amir didn't think that he had a choice. The only other thing he could do would be to climb back down.

Amir paused to gather his strength. He looked up, then down again. He got ready for the challenge.

After a few seconds, he went for it. Amir stepped off with his right foot and moved it up to the new hold. At the same time, he reached his right hand high above his head, trying to grab for another hold.

His foot landed, but his hand did not. His fingers were sore from holding on so tightly. They were too stiff to grab the hold. As his hand slipped off, Amir leaned harder into the side of the wall. A rush of fear ran through his body.

He knew exactly what was happening. He was losing his balance. His hand slid down the side of the wall. His fingers dug into the wall until his fingernails began to tear.

Still, Amir gripped tighter. The harder he tried to find something to hold, the more his fingers hurt. His fingertips were bleeding. Finally, Amir made one last reach for the hold.

This time, he got it. He grabbed on hard. He let out a big sigh. He was safe.

Just then, he felt something touch his left ankle. Amir looked down and saw a hand gripping his leg.

Amir closed his eyes. *Great*, he thought angrily.

- CHAPTER 2 -
SOMETHING TO DO

Amir knew that hand, and that grip, very well. It was Officer Roberts, the police officer who worked in Amir's neighborhood during the week.

"I don't know how many times I need to tell you. You cannot climb the side of this building," came the officer's voice from below. "When are you going to get some sense? One of these times, you are going to get yourself hurt. Or worse!"

If only I had climbed a little higher, Amir thought. *Then he wouldn't have been able to reach me this time.*

But he couldn't do anything about that now. Officer Roberts was not going to let go of his leg unless Amir said he was climbing down.

"Okay, Officer Roberts," Amir said. "I'm coming down."

Officer Roberts let go of Amir's ankle. He stood close by so he could help if Amir started to fall. But coming down from the side of the building was always easier than going up.

Amir got within a few feet of the ground and jumped the rest of the way down. He brushed the dust off his pants. Finally, he looked up at the police officer.

"So tell me, young man, why do you keep trying to climb this building?" Officer Roberts asked.

Amir glanced at the wall beside them. It was a red brick building, just two stories tall. Some of the bricks on the side of the building stuck out. That's what made it a good building to climb.

"I don't know why I like climbing the building," Amir said. "It's just something to do. There's nothing else to do around here."

He and the officer looked around. There were tall apartment buildings everywhere.

The building Amir tried to climb had stores on the first level. Most of the stores were empty. There were apartments above the stores. One of the apartments had broken windows.

Officer Roberts nodded. "I understand," he said. "But I can't let you climb that building. It's too dangerous."

Amir nodded. "I know," he said. "I'm sorry."

Amir was bored a lot of the time. He spent most of his days trying to find things to do. He had to make his own fun.

To Amir, there was nothing more thrilling than climbing that wall.

Officer Roberts noticed the sad look on Amir's face.

"You know what?" the officer said. "You should try to find a place to do some real rock climbing. I think it would be fun for you. Plus, you're good at it."

"How can you tell?" Amir asked.

"Well, in all the years I've been working here, I've never seen anyone try to climb the side of that building," Officer Roberts said. "It's just too hard. Those bricks don't stick out very far, and they aren't very close together. You must be really good to be able to get up higher than my head."

A small grin crossed Amir's face. "Thanks," he said. "I wish there was someplace close I could do it."

Officer Roberts smiled. "I might be able to help you out with that," he said.

- CHAPTER 3 -
OPPORTUNITY

"Look, Amir, you're a good kid," Officer Roberts said. "You're one of the few good ones around here. I'd like to see you stay that way."

Amir smiled.

"I know a place for climbing," Officer Roberts told him. "There is a giant climbing wall inside a store not far from here. They have some one-day classes, and some weeklong classes."

"Where is it?" Amir asked hopefully.

"Woodland Outfitters. It's a huge store right outside the city," Officer Roberts said. "They hook you up with all the right climbing gear, and they help you learn how to climb."

"Oh," Amir said. His head drooped. He knew he'd never be able to go out to the suburbs to a store like that. His mom worked two jobs, and they didn't have a lot of free time together.

"I don't think that will work," Amir said quietly. "My mom won't have time to bring me there."

Officer Roberts smiled. Then he said, "If your mom says it's okay, I'd like to take you out to the store one day this weekend," he said.

Amir looked up at the policeman. "Really?" he asked. "Are you serious? You'd really take me?"

"If your mom says it's okay," the officer said. "I'll stop by after I get done with work and talk to her. But you should warn her that I'm coming. I don't want her to freak out when a policeman shows up at the door!"

They both laughed. "Okay, I will," Amir said. "See you then!"

Amir took off down the street. As he ran home, he got more and more excited. A real climbing wall, with real equipment? It was a dream come true!

He couldn't have been more excited. And he wanted to make sure that his mom would let him do it.

So Amir headed straight home. He got all of his homework done before his mom got home. He even cleaned up his room a bit, too.

When his mom came home, Amir told her what had happened. He had to tell her why he was talking to Officer Roberts in the first place. His mom wasn't too happy to hear that part of the story. But she saw how excited Amir was about climbing the rock wall in the store.

So, when Officer Roberts showed up, Amir's mom agreed to let him go on Saturday.

"My nephew, William, is going to come with us," Officer Roberts said. "He's about the same age as Amir, and he wants to learn how to climb too. So they should get along great."

"Cool," Amir said. He smiled at Officer Roberts. Then he remembered that he wanted to ask the officer some questions.

Amir took a deep breath and asked, "What should I wear? What do I need to bring? How much time will we have there?" The questions came rushing out of him one after another.

Officer Roberts and Amir's mom burst out laughing.

"Relax, Amir," Officer Roberts said. "You can wear whatever you will be comfortable in. You just make sure you stay off that wall on the side of the building, and I'll make sure that Woodland Outfitters has everything all set up for us. See you Saturday."

CHAPTER 4

THE FIRST CLIMB

Officer Roberts showed up right on time at 10 o'clock on Saturday morning. His nephew, William, was with him. William looked as excited as Amir felt about climbing the rock wall.

"This is William," Officer Roberts said. "William, this is Amir."

Amir nervously stretched out his hand to shake William's.

William smiled. "Nice to meet you," he said. "Is this your first time climbing?"

Amir shot Officer Roberts a glance. "Well . . ." Amir began. "Actually, I've been climbing the side of a building a couple of blocks from here. But I've never done real climbing before."

"Really?" William said. "Cool."

They got into Officer Roberts's car. William went on, "There's this huge cliff near my house. They call it Widowmaker. There's a crack about halfway up the side that's big enough to set up camp in."

"That sounds awesome," Amir said.

"I'm going to climb it and camp there sometime," William whispered.

"Wow," Amir said. "That's really cool."

The drive to Woodland Outfitters took about twenty minutes. Finally, Officer Roberts pulled into the store's parking lot and turned the car's engine off.

The store was huge. A big, glass area stuck out from the front of the building. It was almost four stories tall. The largest rock that Amir had ever seen was inside. It was lit up by a thousand lights.

Officer Roberts, Amir, and William walked into the store. The store was packed with outdoor gear. It sold everything from canoes and paddles to badminton sets to snowpants to hunting equipment. But Amir wasn't interested in seeing any of that stuff.

They headed directly for the climbing wall. Officer Roberts went up to the counter. "We're here for climbing lessons," he said, smiling at the man behind the counter.

"Yes," the man said. "Two guys climbing today, right?"

Officer Roberts nodded. "That's right. They're both fourteen," he said.

"Well, we're all ready for you," the man behind the counter said. "And actually, you're in luck. There aren't many people out here today, so you guys can take your time."

"Cool!" William said.

Two instructors came over. Amir's instructor smiled at him. "I'm Ben," he said. "Let's get you into your safety equipment."

Amir stepped into a harness, which was kind of like a belt. It went around Amir's waist and around each of his legs. Ben made sure it was tight.

"We'll attach ropes here," he said, pointing to a large clip in front of Amir's belly. "That's so if you let go of the wall, you won't fall."

"I get it," Amir said. "Cool."

"How much do you weigh?" Ben asked. "I need to know which rope to use to belay for you."

"Belay?" Amir said. "What's that?"

"It really takes two people to climb," Ben said. "One person climbs, and one belays."

"What does the belayer do?" Amir asked.

Ben said, "The person who's belaying stays down below the climber and holds tight to the rope. Then the climber doesn't have to worry about falling. All they have to worry about is climbing."

Ben pointed up to the top of the climbing wall. A rope ran through a large metal clip at the top of the wall.

"The rope will run from your harness, up through that clip, and back down to me," Ben said. "I'll attach it to my harness and wrap it around me so that I can belay you. Your goal is to reach the top. When you get there, you'll see a bell. Ring it, so that everyone knows you made it!"

"You got it," Amir said. "I'm ready!"

William was ready too. He and Amir stood at the bottom of the wall.

"You ready?" William asked.

"Totally," Amir said. "Let's go!"

There were plastic holds spaced all along the side of the wall. There were also a few places along the wall where they could stand.

For the first ten feet or so, the holds were close enough together that the climbing was easy. Amir and William darted up the side of the wall. They raced each other as they went.

With each step Amir took, he could feel Ben pulling in a little of the rope. That way, he wouldn't fall far if he let go of the wall.

About halfway up the wall, the climb got steeper. The holds were farther apart. Amir realized that he had to slow down and think about which way to climb. Sweat beaded up on his forehead as he tried to decide what to do next.

Amir moved a few holds to his right, and William moved to his left. As they got closer together, Amir saw that they were both heading for the same hold.

"Go ahead," Amir told William. "I'll stop here for a second and head up after you." He was being nice, but he also wanted a break to catch his breath.

William smiled and nodded. "Thanks!" he said. He moved for the hold and pulled himself up. He was a little taller than Amir, so the holds were easier for him to get to.

He's so lucky to be tall, Amir thought.

Once William had cleared the hold, Amir continued his climb. The higher he climbed, the more tired he became. His heart pounded and he was sweating.

Finally, Amir was ten feet from the top. His arms and legs were beginning to shake. He was starting to worry that he wouldn't make it.

Down below, Ben was watching.

"Don't worry about climbing down, Amir," Ben yelled up. "Just get to the top. Then I'll teach you how to rappel your way down. It's easy."

Amir frowned. Just then, he heard a noise. It was coming from the top of the rock wall.

Ding! Ding! Ding!

William had beaten him to the top.

· CHAPTER 5 ·
THE FALL

Amir's heart sank. He didn't really care that he hadn't beat William to the top. After all, he had let William go ahead of him. He had almost expected William to reach the top first.

The problem was, he suddenly felt like he couldn't make it, like he couldn't go on. It was the same feeling he'd had when he climbed the building and felt Officer Roberts's hand grab his ankle.

Suddenly, Amir's grip slipped. Since he wasn't holding anything, he slid away from the climbing wall. As he began to free-fall, he let out a yell.

Before he could really scream, the rope attached to his harness went tight. Ben's belaying worked perfectly.

Amir hung in the air, a few feet away from the climbing wall. He felt his face get hot. It seemed like the whole world was staring at him.

Slowly, Ben let out the rope. Amir gently dropped down, closer and closer to the ground.

He glanced over to the other side of the wall. There, William was slowly rappelling down the wall. His instructor was telling him he'd done a great job.

Amir couldn't believe it. He felt like a terrible climber. The day had been a total waste.

Amir reached the ground. He unclipped himself from the belay rope.

"That was great, Amir!" Officer Roberts said. "You almost made it."

"Yeah," Amir said. He looked at the ground and repeated, "Almost." Then he stepped back and watched William rappel down the wall.

"Aren't you going to try again?" Ben asked. "Most kids don't make it as high as you did on their first try."

Amir just shrugged. William got to the bottom of the wall and unhooked himself from the rope. He started to take off his harness.

"You should go again," William said. "You can do it. I didn't make it my first time."

"What do you mean?" Amir asked. "This wasn't your first time?"

"No," William said. "My uncle brings me here whenever I want. I've been up there a bunch of times. You really should try again. I bet you'll make it!"

"I'm too tired," Amir said. "Maybe next time."

Ben walked over, smiling. "That was a great first day, Amir," he said. "I hope you can come back sometime. Before you leave, stop back by the counter. I have something for you."

"Okay," Amir said. "Thanks for everything."

Amir, William, and Officer Roberts spent the next hour walking around the store. Officer Roberts wanted to pick up some tennis balls, and they looked at fishing and camping gear, too.

Soon, it was time to head back to the city. On their way out, Amir, William, and Officer Roberts stopped at the climbing wall.

"Here, take this," Ben said. He handed a colorful piece of paper to Amir. "We're having a climbing camp this summer," Ben went on. "It's here at the store, eight hours a day for a week. The price includes all the gear you need. You guys would love it. Lots of rock climbing!"

"Awesome!" William said, looking at the piece of paper. "I really want to go."

"Me too," Amir said.

* * *

When Amir got home that night, he had forgotten about being disappointed that he hadn't reached the top. He found his mom in the kitchen.

He told her about climbing the wall, and how he had almost reached the top. He told her what a great climber William was. He asked if he could go back with Officer Roberts again someday.

Finally, he told her about the climbing camp. He nervously handed his mom the piece of paper.

Amir's mom looked at the paper. "It looks fun, but it's a lot of money," she said. She looked at Amir and saw the excitement in his eyes.

"Mom, I'll earn money to pay for half of it myself," Amir said. "And I'll get all my homework done without having to be asked. And I'll keep my room clean. And—"

Finally, his mom smiled. "Okay, okay," she said. "We'll figure out a way to pay for it."

Amir leaped in the air.

- CHAPTER 6 -
CHANGE OF PLANS

The three months before climbing camp started seemed like the longest three months of Amir's life. But he stayed pretty busy, keeping all the promises he'd made to his mom.

He earned some money by running errands for other families in his building after school and on weekends. Sometimes he had to go to the grocery store for them, or pick up laundry at the laundromat.

He did his homework every night after dinner. In fact, his grades even improved. And he kept his room clean most of the time.

William was going to camp too. He and Amir kept in touch online. They made plans to ride to the store together every day for camp, and talked about all the things they'd learn.

Amir had never been so excited. He couldn't wait for climbing camp.

About a month before camp started, Amir ran into Officer Roberts outside his apartment building.

"Hi, Amir. Well, I guess you heard the bad news about William," Officer Roberts said.

"What do you mean?" Amir asked.

"Oh, I thought he told you," Officer Roberts said. "William is not going to be able to go to climbing camp with you."

Amir was shocked. "I just got a text message from him yesterday!" he said. "He didn't tell me anything was wrong."

"Well, it seems like William is doing some dangerous climbing, just like you used to," the officer said. "He got caught trying to free climb some big rock out by his house. He fell and almost broke his neck. He's fine, but his parents grounded him for six months. Including climbing camp."

Widowmaker, Amir thought. His heart sank.

Amir sent William a text message on his way home, but William didn't respond.

Three weeks went by, and Amir didn't hear anything from his friend. Finally, the night before the first day of camp, Amir got a text message.

"Have fun," was all it said.

Amir replied, but William didn't say anything else.

* * *

Camp was amazing.

Every day, Officer Roberts or Amir's mom drove him to the outdoor store. There, Amir and ten other guys his age learned everything there was to learn about rock climbing.

By the end of the first day, Amir had reached the top of the rock wall and rung the bell.

On the last day of camp, the instructors brought all the students to a real climbing cliff an hour out of town. Real climbers regularly climbed the cliff, so there were climbing bolts already in place.

Climbing the cliff was one of the scariest times of Amir's life, but when he reached the top, he felt great.

The class had a picnic on the top of the giant rock. Then they rappelled down the cliff and headed home.

Amir didn't hear from William until summer was almost over. Then, one afternoon, they were both online at the same time. Amir sent William an instant message.

AMIRCLIMBER: Long time no talk!

ROCKWALLWILLIAM: Yeah, busy.

AMIRCLIMBER: Too bad you couldn't come to camp. It was so cool. Plus now I have my own rock-climbing gear!

ROCKWALLWILLIAM: Big deal. Free climbing is better.

AMIRCLIMBER: With this equipment and me belaying, you could climb Widowmaker no problem.

ROCKWALLWILLIAM: I don't need equipment to climb.

AMIRCLIMBER: r u going to free climb it again?

AMIRCLIMBER: r u?

AMIRCLIMBER: R U???

ROCKWALLWILLIAM has signed off.

- CHAPTER 7 -
MISSING WILLIAM

Amir couldn't believe it. William was climbing Widowmaker with no safety gear.

He knew he should tell Officer Roberts, but he didn't want to. William might get into trouble. Amir didn't want that to happen. But if William climbed the cliff, he could seriously hurt himself.

Amir couldn't sleep that night. Every time he dozed off, he started thinking about William climbing Widowmaker.

Amir remembered the feeling he had the first time he went to the climbing wall, when he slipped off. That horrible feeling of falling ended when the belay rope was pulled. But when a person free climbed, there was no rope to save them.

After tossing and turning for hours, Amir finally fell asleep. When he woke up the next morning, he suddenly knew exactly what he needed to do. He needed to help William.

As he brushed his teeth, he heard a knock at the front door. He swung the door open. Officer Roberts was standing there. He looked upset.

"Amir, I need your help," the officer said. "It's William. He's missing."

"Missing?" Amir said.

"Yes," Officer Roberts replied. "His mother said he wasn't home when she woke up this morning. And he's been gone all day."

Amir took a deep breath. "I think I might know where he is," he said. "Do you know where that big cliff is that he climbs?"

Officer Roberts nodded. "I think so, yes," he said. "But William knows he is not to go near that. He got in so much trouble last time he was there. Plus, he could have died. I don't think he'd go back."

"I do," Amir said. "If you take me there, I think I can help."

- CHAPTER 8 -
TO THE RESCUE

Amir quickly went to his room. He put all of his climbing gear into a bag. He wrote a note to his mom, telling her what was happening and where he would be. Then he and Officer Roberts left.

Officer Roberts turned on the lights on his police car. They drove out to the town where William lived. It was about thirty minutes away from Amir's apartment building.

On the way, Amir told the officer about the instant messages from William the night before. Officer Roberts looked worried.

"I'm pretty sure he's trying to climb Widowmaker," Amir said. "And I know he's doing it without equipment."

Officer Roberts sighed. "It sure sounds like it," he said. "I just hope we can make it in time."

Soon, Officer Roberts parked his squad car at the base of a steep cliff. Amir couldn't believe his eyes. The cliff had no slope at all — it was a sheer wall of rock that stretched up for what seemed like miles.

There were some rocks sticking out that a person could use to free climb, but Amir didn't think there were enough.

Plus, the cliff was hard and rough. Any fall down the side of the cliff, even just sliding down the rough surface, could hurt someone.

Amir walked around the base of the cliff, looking up.

"What are you doing?" Officer Roberts asked.

"I'm looking for something," Amir said.

"Looking for what?" Officer Roberts asked.

"William told me about a crack in the cliff," Amir said. "He said it was big enough to hide in. There! There it is!"

Amir pointed up. Officer Roberts looked up the side of the cliff. He saw a large crack in the side of the rock, about halfway up.

"That's where he is, I bet," Amir said.

"All the way up there?" Officer Roberts said quietly. "That's so dangerous."

"William!" Amir yelled. "Are you up there?"

A soft voice called back. "That was him," Officer Roberts said. "I'm sure of it." He headed toward his squad car. "I'm calling the fire department," he said.

"Wait! What's that?" Amir asked. He pointed at the side of the rocky cliff, about ten feet above their heads. "Is that what I think it is?"

Officer Roberts asked, "What is it?"

Without another word, Amir ran to the squad car and grabbed his climbing equipment. Then he started getting into his harness.

Before long, he was all strapped up, with ropes attached, and wearing his helmet.

"What do you think you're doing?" Officer Roberts asked. "I don't need two of you crazy kids stuck up there. There's no way I'm letting you do this, Amir."

Amir stopped. He stared at Officer Roberts. "Officer Roberts," he said politely, "here's the deal. No fire truck's ladder can reach that high. And that thing right there, sticking out from the cliff? That's a bolt. A climbing bolt. Do you know what that means?"

Officer Roberts's frown turned into a smile. "Yes, I do," he said. "It means that real climbers use this cliff."

"Exactly," Amir said. "And they do it the right way. That's what I'm going to do."

Officer Roberts quickly called for an ambulance and the fire department to help them.

"You should tell them to bring an extra harness," Amir said. "I have an extra one, but you need to wear it so that we can attach my rope to you."

"Got it," Officer Roberts said.

"Just make sure to keep the rope tight," Amir added. "With each climb I make, you'll have to pull a little bit, to make sure the rope will hold me if I fall. And I have an extra rope, so we can help William get down."

"Okay," Officer Roberts said.

Amir started up the side of the rock. He left one end of the rope for Officer Roberts to use to belay for him.

As he climbed, Amir moved from one bolt to another. At each new bolt, he hooked up the belay rope. After only a few minutes, he had reached the huge crack in the side of the rock.

· CHAPTER 9 ·
BOLTED

William had described an opening big
enough to set up camp in. But the crack
only went back a few feet. It was barely big
enough to sit in. Amir couldn't imagine
anyone sleeping in there. It wasn't at all
what he'd expected.

But William was inside. He was sitting
back against the rock. His eyes were huge.
Amir could tell that he was scared out of
his mind.

Amir reached for his friend. "Come on," Amir said. "Let's go back down."

Instead of reaching back, William clung tighter to the rock. "No!" William shouted.

Amir frowned. "Come on, William," he said. "It's not safe up here."

William shook his head. "I can't move," he said quietly.

"What happened? Are you okay?" Amir asked. He leaned over to see if William was bleeding.

"I'm not hurt," William said. "I got up here last night, and when I saw that there wasn't a cave, I just freaked out. Now I'm too scared to go down."

"I got you, bud," Amir said. "Guess what? This rock's bolted!"

Amir leaned out of the crack. Emergency workers were gathered below. "Send up another harness," Amir called. He dropped one end of his extra rope down.

Soon, Amir pulled up a harness for William. William slipped it on without standing up.

While William got ready, Amir ran his extra rope through a bolt in the rock. Then he clipped it to William's harness.

Amir leaned out of the crack again. He dropped the other end of the rope down to one of the firefighters.

"There," Amir said. "You're all set. The big guys are down at the bottom. They're ready to help us get down. All you need to do is rappel down, just like at the climbing wall."

"Okay," William said nervously. Then he asked, "Is this what you learned at climbing camp?"

"Yeah," Amir said. "And if you ever stop climbing things you shouldn't be climbing, you can learn that stuff too."

Both boys laughed. As they got ready to head down the cliff, William looked over at Amir. "Next year," he said, "I'm there."

Then they slowly headed onto the face of the cliff.

ABOUT THE AUTHOR

Bob Temple lives in Rosemount, Minnesota, with his wife and three children. He has written more than thirty books for children. Over the years, he has coached more than twenty kids' soccer, basketball, and baseball teams. He also loves visiting classrooms to talk about his writing.

ABOUT THE ILLUSTRATOR

When Sean Tiffany was growing up, he lived on a small island off the coast of Maine. Every day, from sixth grade until he graduated from high school, he had to take a boat to get to school. When Sean isn't working on his art, he works on a multimedia project called "OilCan Drive," which combines music and art. He has a pet cactus named Jim.

GLOSSARY

belay (buh-LAY)—in climbing, to secure a rope to the climber and to a person on the ground so that the climber does not fall

equipment (i-KWIP-muhnt)—the tools needed for a particular purpose

experience (ek-SPEER-ee-uhnss)—skill or knowledge

harness (HAR-niss)—an arrangement of straps worn around the body to keep someone safe

hold (HOHLD)—something that is grabbed or held on to for support

muscles (MUHSS-uhlz)—the parts of your body that produce movement

rappel (rah-PEL)—to climb down a vertical surface using a rope

surface (SUR-fiss)—the outside or outermost layer of something

unnecessary (uhn-NESS-uh-ser-ee)—not needed

vertical (VER-tuh-kuhl)—upright, or straight up and down

MORE ABOUT ROCK CLIMBING

Rock climbing looks like lots of fun, but it can be extremely dangerous. Just like Amir and William learned, you should never try to climb a cliff or rock without proper training and equipment. You should be able to find rock climbing classes in your area by looking on the Internet. Of course, be sure to have adult permission before signing up for any classes.

There are many different types of rock climbing. Here are some examples:

* **Ice Climbing:** Instead of climbing a rock, climbers use picks, special shoes, and axes to help them climb giant walls of ice.

* **Indoor Climbing:** Climbing on a man-made wall inside a building. It's a great way to learn how to climb from experts.

* **Solo Climbing:** Free climbing all alone, with no ropes or protection. It's the most dangerous type of climbing.

* **Traditional Climbing:** Climbers usually go in groups or pairs, with each climber having another person belay for them. In traditional climbing, there are no permanent holds for the climber to use. They must insert and secure all of their own holds on the climb, or use natural holds on the rock's surface to help them.

* **Sport Climbing:** Just like traditional climbing, except climbers use holds that are permanently attached to the surface of the rock (like the bolts Amir found on Widowmaker in this story).

DISCUSSION QUESTIONS

1. Was it wrong for William to climb Widowmaker without equipment?

2. Why did Officer Roberts offer to take Amir to the climbing wall in the beginning of this book?

3. Did Amir do the right thing when he told Officer Roberts that he thought William was at Widowmaker?

WRITING PROMPTS

1. Pretend that you're Amir. Write a journal entry about your experience at climbing camp.

2. In this book, William broke the rules when he climbed Widowmaker, and he almost got badly hurt. Have you ever broken the rules and put yourself in danger? Write about it. What happened?

3. In the beginning of this book, Amir climbed buildings because he was bored. What do you do when you're bored?

OTHER BOOKS

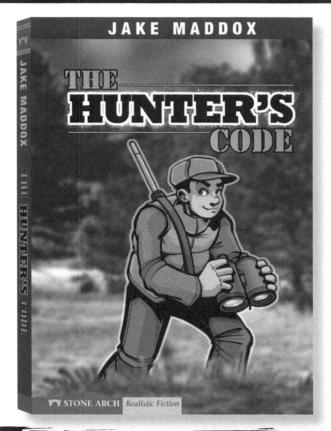

On a hunt with his dad, Ethan discovers some dead deer left in the woods. A poacher is killing the animals for fun. Ethan knows that's against the Hunter's Code — after all, he broke that rule himself.

BY JAKE MADDOX

Nick has always loved camping, but his cousins don't listen to his warnings about campfires and bears, and they make fun of everything Nick does. When Devin finds himself in real danger, can Nick save him in time?

INTERNET SITES

Do you want to know more about subjects related to this book? Or are you interested in learning about other topics? Then check out FactHound, a fun, easy way to find Internet sites.

Our investigative staff has already sniffed out great sites for you!

Here's how to use FactHound:

1. Visit *www.facthound.com*

2. Select your grade level.

3. To learn more about subjects related to this book, type in the book's ISBN number: **9781434207845**.

4. Click the **Fetch It** button.

FactHound will fetch the best Internet sites for you!